THE BURGLAR'S BREAKFAST

Felicity Everett

Illustrated by Christyan Fox

Designed by Maria Wheatley

Language and Reading Consultant: David Wray
(Education Department, University of Exeter, England)

Series Editor: Gaby Waters

First published in 1995 by Usborne Publishing Ltd, Usborne House, 83-85 Saffron Hill, London EC1N 8RT, England. Copyright © 1994 Usborne Publishing Ltd.

Alfie Briggs was a burglar.

He wasn't very good at burgling, though.

Tonight Alfie had stolen

a broken lawn mower
a hat rack
and a talking bird.

After a hard night's thieving, Alfie liked to go home to a tasty breakfast.

It was his main meal of the day, so he ate at least five courses.

And he tried to make sure he never ran out of his top five breakfast foods.

Can you guess what they were?

He followed the trail around the corner and into the park.

Where had the thief gone next?

On his way home,
Alfie thought about
what he'd have instead.

Just then
Alfie noticed
a broken egg shell
beside the hedge.

Can you guess who that someone was?

Alfie bent down and peeped through the hole in the hedge.

On the other side of the hole were two more egg shells...

...and one happy fox.

Been raiding Farmer Till's chickens have you? Ha ha. Good luck to you.

But as the fox cub ran off home,
Alfie spotted something.

The little rascal.
Those eggs weren't
Farmer Till's at all,
they were mine!

How could Alfie tell?

11

Right, it will have to be trout then.

Alfie flung open the door of the refrigerator – only to find an empty plate where the trout had been.

This is getting beyond a joke.

Alfie's patience was wearing thin.

But this time he had a good idea who the thief was.

Do *you* think
Tibbles was the thief?

Alfie set the table,
  turned on the oven and
    went to get his waffles.

Someone had been there
first. And this time the trail
led to a mousehole.

The mice hadn't *eaten* Alfie's waffles.
What had they done with them?

If you look closely,
you might be able to spot the
sneaky low-down creeps yourself.

Alfie needed his magnifying glass to solve this one.

By the time he'd worked it out, there wasn't a grain of sugar left.

Alfie felt helpless and cross.

Oh dear! Maybe this was how people felt when he burgled their houses.

He was ashamed.

20

But even one of Rosie's special breakfasts couldn't cheer Alfie up.

I don't want to be a burglar anymore. But I don't know how to do anything else...

...or do I?

Something had given Alfie an idea.
Can you see what it was?

Alfie picked up the paper for a closer look.

NEED A JOB?
Can you:
Follow trails?
Track down stolen goods?
Catch crooks?
Spot clues?
Keep a cool head?
The STOP-A-THIEF Detective
Agency needs YOU!

Follow trails.

Track down stolen goods.

The Stop-A-Thief Detective Agency had never known anything like it.

Alfie caught more crooks in his first week than all the other detectives put together.

Caught red-handed!

And he never stole another thing – not even breakfast.